Watch Out, William!

Written by Nette Hilton
Illustrated by Beth Norling

An easy-to-read SOLO
for beginning readers

SOLOS

Southwood Books Limited
4 Southwood Lawn Road
London N6 5SF

First published in Australia by Omnibus Books 1998

Published in the UK under licence from
Omnibus Books by
Southwood Books Limited, 2001

This edition produced for The Book People Ltd.,
Hall Wood Avenue, Haydock, St Helens WA11 9UL

Text copyright © Nette Hilton 1998
Illustrations copyright © Beth Norling 1998

Cover design by Lyn Mitchell

ISBN 1 903207 22 3

Printed in Hong Kong

A CIP catalogue record for this book is available
from the British Library

For Melissa, a cyclist of style – N.H.

For Chris and Rosa – B.N.

Chapter 1

William had a fine bike. It was a bright yellow BMX. The bell on the handlebar gave a loud *ding! ding!* and the tyres were big and fat.

William couldn't ride his bike very well yet. He could walk with it, but it wobbled and bumped when he tried to get on.

His mum and dad gave him a gold bike helmet with a big flash of lightning down the side. William wore it in the garden while he walked his bike.

Soon William could ride his bike in the garden and along the path at the side of the house.

When he felt a little braver, he rode very slowly all the way down to the corner shop.

The shopkeeper, Mr Purvis, was a friend of his.

"Watch out, William!" said Mr Purvis as William wobbled past, nearly crashing into a pile of boxes.

"Oh dear," said William.

Mr Purvis smiled. "Don't worry," he said. "Before long you'll be riding like an Olympic champion."

Chapter 2

More than anything, William wanted to ride his bike to school. But it was a very long way, and he wasn't sure he was ready to ride that far.

What if there was a hole or a post in a place where it hadn't been before? His teacher, Miss Samson, wouldn't like it if he arrived at school late, or muddy.

He decided that it would be much easier to *walk* the bike to school. And he did just that!

When it was time to go home, William was worried all over again. Should he walk his bike, or ride it?

Miss Samson made up his mind for him. "Hop in the bike line, William," she said. "And when I say *Go*, you pedal out the gate."

William hopped on his bike.

"Go!" yelled Miss Samson.

Chapter 3

William took a deep breath. He pointed his bike to the left and pushed hard on the pedal. But he didn't see the big rock near his front wheel.

The bike didn't go left. It went right. Straight up the ramp of a cattle truck.

"*Moo!*" said Bessie the cow.

The truck driver, Mr Swats, wheeled William down the ramp and gave him back his helmet.

"You'll be OK now," he said. "Watch out for any more trucks!"

William held on tight to the handlebars and started to pedal. He was so busy watching out for trucks that he didn't notice where his bike was going.

It was taking him along the steep downhill side of the roundabout.

Chapter 4

Mrs Peach was standing at the top of the hill with baby Imogen in her pram. She was talking to Mrs Max and her dog Zeff.

Bounce, bounce, bounce went baby Imogen while she waited for her mother.

Rock, rock, rock went the pram.

Twang! went the brake on the
pram as it came loose.

Away went the pram, and away went baby Imogen, faster and faster down the hill.

"My baby!" cried Mrs Peach. "Help! Somebody please save my baby!"

Faster went the pram down the pavement. Faster went William down the road. Faster and faster they both flew as the hill got steeper and steeper.

The bike rattled and shook, and the pram thumped and bumped.

William didn't fall off when Zeff tried to grab his wheel.

He didn't fall off when he bounced
over a huge hole in the road.

He didn't even fall off when his bike jumped up off the road and on to the pavement.

He hung on tight and just kept going.

Chapter 5

"Ga-ga-ga!" sang baby Imogen when she saw William racing up beside her.

By now William had stopped watching out for trucks.

He could hardly see at all, because the wind had made his eyes fill with tears. But he knew that something white and bouncy was rushing along very close to him. He could hear it talking.

"Bubba-bubba-bubba!" it said. "*Wheeeee!*"

William tried hard to see what it was. He put out a foot to feel it. Then he pulled his foot back – or tried to.

"Ooooooohhhhh!" said William.
He opened his eyes very wide.

His shoe lace was stuck in the side of a big white baby pram, and inside the pram was baby Imogen Peach.

Chapter 6

"Help!" called Mrs Peach from a long way up the hill. "Somebody save my Imogen!"

William saw a very big baker's van in front of the corner shop. A wide wooden ramp led out of its back door.

William looked hard at the ramp.
He knew exactly what to do.

"Hold on, Imogen!" he cried.

He leaned to one side, and he and the bike and Imogen and the pram all flew across the pavement, over the kerb, on to the road, up the ramp, and right into the back of the very big baker's van.

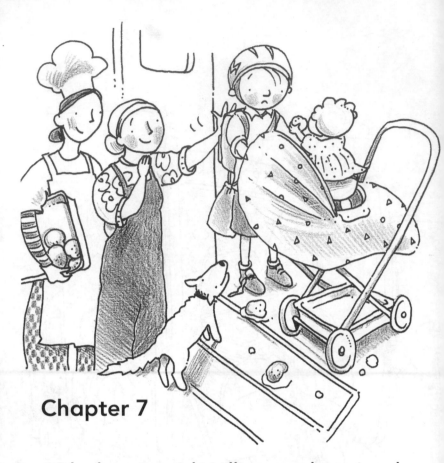

Chapter 7

"Oh dear," said William as he wiped a jam roll off the seat of his shorts.

"Oh dear," he said again as he took three cream buns away from

baby Imogen. "Oh dear, oh dear."
But nobody else seemed to mind.

"Hooray!" cried the van driver.
"What a hero!"

"Bravo!" cried Mrs Peach, as she
gave William a big hug. "You saved
my baby!"

William looked at baby Imogen. She had a round dob of cream on her nose. "I saved you," he said.

"Wheeeeee!" said baby Imogen.

William watched as Mrs Peach and baby Imogen and a lot of cream buns set off up the hill. Baby Imogen waved to him all the way.

Chapter 8

Mr Purvis held the bike ready for William to climb on.

"Well done, William," he said. "I knew you could do it! You rode your bike just like one of those Olympic champions!"

William was very happy. He stretched his legs out and did four little springy jumps, just like real champions do.

"Thank you, Mr Purvis," he said as he climbed back on his bike.

He put his foot firmly on the
pedal and smiled at the small crowd
in front of the corner shop.

As he pedalled away, he lifted his hand to wave.

Almost.

Nette Hilton

When I was young I wasn't very brave about riding my bike. I liked to ride close to fences so I could hold on if the wheels went one way and I looked like going another.

I can still remember the very first time I took one hand off the handlebar to wave to my friend. And I can still remember the very first time my bike took off and raced down the steepest hill in town. The wind rushed by so fast that all the world was a great big blur.

Writing about it was much more fun than doing it!

Beth Norling

I remember Dad teaching me how to ride a bike. I sat on the bike while he held on to the back of the seat. He ran, still holding on to the seat, and I pedalled. I was a bit like William and very nervous, so when I found out that I was riding along and Dad was no longer helping, I fell off!

Now I just get around on things with four wheels, but I can't wait till my baby is big enough to ride his tricycle.

More Solos!

Dog Star
Janeen Brian and Ann James

The Best Pet
Penny Matthews and Beth Norling

Fuzz the Famous Fly
Emily Rodda and Tom Jellett

Cat Chocolate
Kate Darling and Mitch Vane

Green Fingers
Emily Rodda and Craig Smith

Gabby's Fair
Robin Klein and Michael Johnson

Watch Out William
Nette Hilton and Beth Norling

The Great Jimbo James
Phil Cummings and David Cox